This Walker book

belongs to:

........................................................

........................................................

*To Jo and Daniel, with love* ◇ T. K.

*For Xander William Higgins* ◇ P. B.

First published 2015 by Walker Books Ltd 87 Vauxhall Walk, London SE11 5HJ • 10 9 8 7 6 5 4 3 2 1
This edition published 2016 • Text © 2015 Timothy Knapman • Illustrations © 2015 Patrick Benson • The right of Timothy Knapman
and Patrick Benson to be identified as author and illustrator respectively of this work has been asserted by them in accordance with
the Copyright Designs and Patents Act 1988 • This book has been typeset in Olde Claude LP Regular • Printed in China • All rights
reserved. No part of this book may be reproduced, transmitted or stored in an information retrieval system in any form or by any means,
graphic, electronic or mechanical, including photocopying taping and recording, without prior written permission from the publisher
British Library Cataloguing in Publication Data: a catalogue record for this book is available from the British Library
ISBN 978-1-4063-6566-5 • www.walker.co.uk

# Soon

WALKER BOOKS
AND SUBSIDIARIES
LONDON · BOSTON · SYDNEY · AUCKLAND

Timothy Knapman

illustrated by Patrick Benson

Very early one morning,
Raju and his mummy set out
on a great adventure.
It was cold and dark.
They walked for a long time.

"When can we go home again?"
asked Raju.

"Soon," said his mummy.

They came to the river,
where the crocodiles dozed.

"We must be very quiet,"
said Raju's mummy.

But the crocodiles heard them
anyway and came snapping.

Raju's mummy stamped her feet
so hard it made the ground tremble.

And the crocodiles went scrambling
off into the water.

"When can we go home again?"
asked Raju.

"Soon,"
said his mummy.

They came to the forest,
where the snake sleeps.

"We must be very quiet,"
said Raju's mummy.

But the snake heard them
anyway and came slithering.

Raju's mummy blew her trunk
so hard it made
the trees shake.

And the snake went
sliding off into the shadows.

"When can we go home again?"
asked Raju.

"Soon,"
said his mummy.

They came to the tall grass,
where the tiger prowled.

"We must be very quiet,"
said Raju's mummy.

But the tiger heard them anyway
and came roaring.

Raju's mummy reared up so high
she was as tall as a giant.

And the tiger went running off
into the tall grass.

"When can we go home again?"
asked Raju.

"Soon," said his mummy.

Then they came to the mountain.

"We're going to climb it,"
said Raju's mummy.
"Hold on tight to my tail."

At last they reached the top of the mountain.
Raju could see all his world spread out before him.

"It's beautiful, isn't it?"
said Raju's mummy.

"Yes," said Raju.

They were very quiet.

"When can we go
home again?" asked Raju.

His mummy smiled
and stroked his head
with her trunk.

"Now," she said.

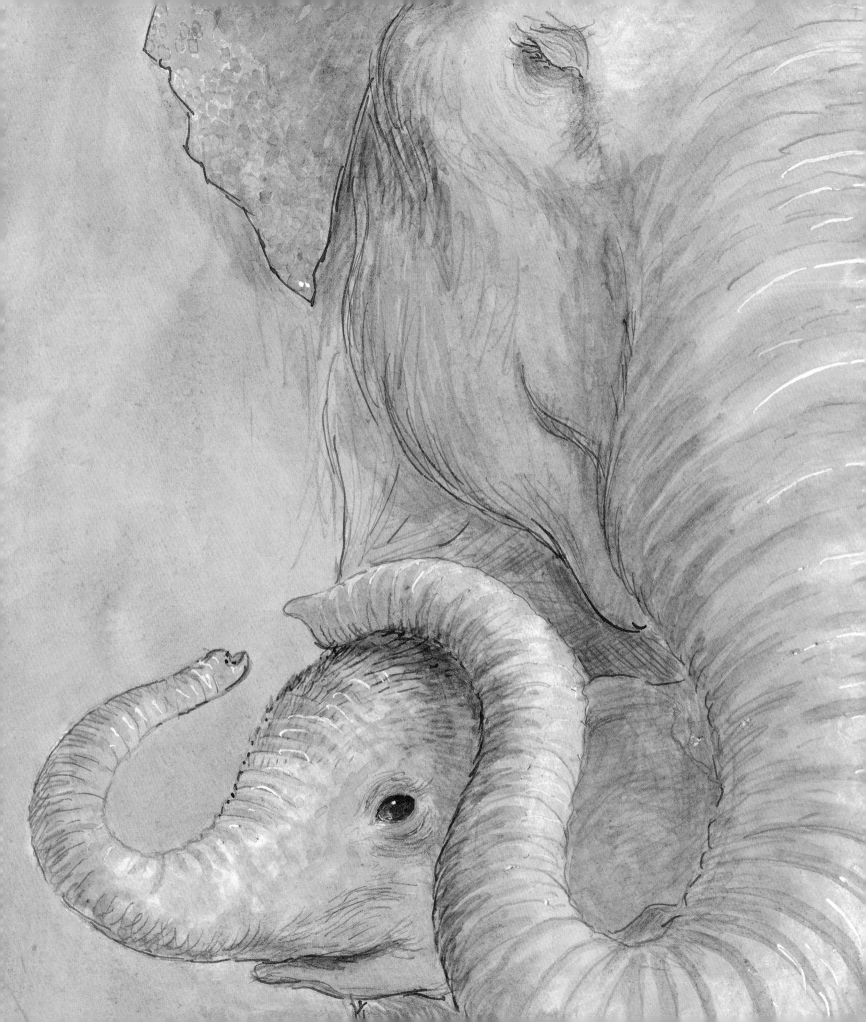

And they walked all the way back down the mountain ...

   past the tiger in the tall grass ...
past the snake in the forest ...
   past the crocodiles by the river ...

to their snug little home.

"Did you enjoy our great adventure?"
asked Raju's mummy.

Raju was tired and his feet hurt
and he'd never been up so late
in his life before.

"When can we do it all again?"
Raju said.

"Soon,"

said his mummy.

**TIMOTHY KNAPMAN** is a children's writer, lyricist and playwright. His children's books have been translated into twelve languages and published all over the world. His titles have often been featured on CBeebies Bedtime Stories. *Soon* is his debut to the Walker Books list. He lives in Surrey.

**PATRICK BENSON** is the illustrator of the beloved and best-selling *Owl Babies* by Martin Waddell and has also illustrated books by Roald Dahl and Russell Hoban, among others. He has won many awards including a Mother Goose Award, a Christopher Award, and a Kurt Maschler Award. He lives in Scotland.

Available from all good booksellers

www.walker.co.uk